Dear Parent:
Your child's love of reading starts here!

Every child learns to read in a different way and at his or her own speed. Some go back and forth between reading levels and read favorite books again and again. Others read through each level in order. You can help your young reader improve and become more confident by encouraging his or her own interests and abilities. From books your child reads with you to the first books he or she reads alone, there are I Can Read Books for every stage of reading:

SHARED READING
Basic language, word repetition, and whimsical illustrations, ideal for sharing with your emergent reader

BEGINNING READING
Short sentences, familiar words, and simple concepts for children eager to read on their own

READING WITH HELP
Engaging stories, longer sentences, and language play for developing readers

READING ALONE
Complex plots, challenging vocabulary, and high-interest topics for the independent reader

ADVANCED READING
Short paragraphs, chapters, and exciting themes for the perfect bridge to chapter books

I Can Read Books have introduced children to the joy of reading since 1957. Featuring award-winning authors and illustrators and a fabulous cast of beloved characters, I Can Read Books set the standard for beginning readers.

A lifetime of discovery begins with the magical words "I Can Read!"

Visit www.icanread.com for information
on enriching your child's reading experience.

Sumaya and Roger chalk up another one!
—H. P.

For Skip and Debbie, with love
—L. A.

Gouache and black pencil were used to prepare the full-color art.

I Can Read Book® is a trademark of HarperCollins Publishers.
Amelia Bedelia is a registered trademark of Peppermint Partners, LLC.

Amelia Bedelia Chalks One Up. Text copyright © 2014 by Herman S. Parish III. Illustrations copyright © 2014 by Lynne Avril. All rights reserved. No part of this book may be used or reproduced in any manner whatsoever without written permission except in the case of brief quotations embodied in critical articles and reviews. Printed in the United States of America. For information address HarperCollins Children's Books, a division of HarperCollins Publishers, 195 Broadway, New York, NY 10007. www.icanread.com

Library of Congress Cataloging-in-Publication Data
Parish, Herman.
Amelia Bedelia chalks one up / Herman Parish ; pictures by Lynne Avril.
    pages cm—(I can read. Level 1)
"Greenwillow Books."
Summary: Amelia Bedelia wants her mother to stop feeling blue. She suggests Mom go on a playdate while Amelia Bedelia is doing the same, and then enlists her friends to help make chalk drawings on the house, sidewalk, and more to brighten Mom's day with her favorite things.
ISBN 978-0-06-233422-0 (hardback)—ISBN 978-0-06-233421-3 (pbk.) [1. Mood (Psychology)—Fiction.
2. Drawing—Fiction. 3. Mothers and daughters—Fiction. 4. Humorous stories.] I. Avril, Lynne, (date) illustrator. II. Title.
PZ7.P2185Aob 2014 [E]—dc23 2014010789

14 15 16 17 LP/WOR 10 9 8 7 6 5 4 3 2 1 First Edition
Greenwillow Books

I Can Read!

BEGINNING 1 READING

Amelia Bedelia
·Chalks One Up·

by Herman Parish ❀ pictures by Lynne Avril

Greenwillow Books, *An Imprint of* HarperCollins*Publishers*

Amelia Bedelia's mother
was as glum as the weather.
"Where is the sun?" she asked.
"I am really blue."

Amelia Bedelia looked at her mother.

She was not blue.

She was not even wearing anything blue.

She was not wearing a smile, either.

"I am having a playdate,"
said Amelia Bedelia.
"Maybe you should have one, too."

"Great idea, sweetie!"

said Amelia Bedelia's mom.

She made two short phone calls.

Then she said,

"I am going to town.

After I go shopping,

I will meet Dad for coffee.

Mrs. Adams will watch you and Rose."

"Have fun," said Mrs. Adams,

who was their next-door neighbor.

"Don't worry about us girls.

We will have a ball."

Amelia Bedelia's mother
waved good-bye.
"Well, chalk up another gray day!"
she said.
As Amelia Bedelia waved back,
she got an even better idea.

Amelia Bedelia found
her big bucket of chalk
in the garage.

When Rose's father dropped Rose off,
Amelia Bedelia was
already hard at work.

"Wow!" said Rose.
"You have every color
in the rainbow!"

"I need them," said Amelia Bedelia.

"I'm chalking up a gray day

to make my mom happy.

Want to help?"

"Sure!" said Rose.

To warm up their drawing arms,
Amelia Bedelia and Rose drew
squares for hopscotch
on the sidewalk.
When they played a game,
Mrs. Adams was amazing!

15

Chip walked by with his big brother
and their puppy, Scout.

"What is going on?" yelled Chip.

"We're chalking up a gray day,"
said Amelia Bedelia.

"Want to help?"

"Cool!" said Chip.

16

"What makes your mom happy?"
asked Rose.
"She likes flowers and green things,"
said Amelia Bedelia,
pointing to where plants grew last year.

Rose got green, red, and pink chalk.

She began drawing roses

on Amelia Bedelia's house.

"Hey, Amelia Bedelia!"
Daisy was walking by
with her babysitter
and her baby sister.
"What are you doing?" she asked.
"Chalking up a gray day,"
said Amelia Bedelia.
"Want to help?"
"Yes!" said Daisy.

Daisy began drawing daisies.

"That's my mom's favorite flower,"

said Amelia Bedelia.

"She will love those.

Thanks!"

20

Amelia Bedelia told her friends

about her mom's favorite spots.

Chip drew a map.

Amelia Bedelia, Rose, and Daisy

added shops and places to eat.

Library

Bridge!! Bridge!!

PET STORE

Pete's Diner

23

Mrs. Adams made tasty treats

for everyone.

"What great drawings," she said.

"Roll out the red carpet for your mom!"

Amelia Bedelia didn't have one.
So they drew her mom a carpet
leading to the best surprise of all.

Then Amelia Bedelia saw their car
pulling into the driveway.
Her parents had come home together.
"Hi, Mom!" said Amelia Bedelia.
"Welcome back!"

"You guys really went to town,"
said Amelia Bedelia's father.
"Not us," said Amelia Bedelia.
"Mom went to town.
We stayed home and drew!"

Amelia Bedelia's parents
followed the red carpet.
Everyone else followed them.
"A yellow sun plus a blue mom
makes green," said Amelia Bedelia.
"And green makes you happy."

Amelia Bedelia's mother

was speechless.

She hugged each of them.

She hugged Amelia Bedelia

the longest of all.

Amelia Bedelia's dad

took more photographs.

It was a good thing he did.

It rained all night long.

The chalk washed away,

and the pictures melted.

All the colors of the rainbow

soaked into the earth.

The next day was bright and sunny.

Amelia Bedelia and her mom

stood at the window

feeling yellow and pink and green

and every other color . . . except blue.